MONTY

by James Stevenson

 Greenwillow Books, New York

LIBRARY OF CONGRESS CATALOGING-IN-PUBLICATION DATA
STEVENSON, JAMES (DATE)
MONTY / BY JAMES STEVENSON.
P.   CM.
SUMMARY: THE RABBIT, DUCK, AND FROG FIND THAT
THEY HAVE NO WAY TO CROSS THE RIVER WHEN THEIR
ALLIGATOR FRIEND, MONTY, TAKES A VACATION.
ISBN 0-688-11241-2 (RTE)
[1. ALLIGATORS—FICTION.   2. ANIMALS—FICTION.
3. CARTOONS AND COMICS.]   I. TITLE.
PZ7.S84748MON   1992
[E]—DC20   91-20657   CIP   AC

To Jane Walker Stevenson

EVERY MORNING, ARTHUR AND
DORIS AND TOM WALKED TO
SCHOOL TOGETHER.
WHEN THEY CAME TO THE WIDE
RIVER, THEY LOOKED FOR MONTY.

MONTY WAS ALWAYS ASLEEP, SNORING.
WAKE UP, MONTY! THIS IS A SCHOOL DAY!
GUG... GUGGLE.. GORGA... GUG...

THEY CLIMBED ON
MONTY'S BACK, AND
HE SWAM ACROSS
THE RIVER.

WHEN THEY GOT TO THE FAR SIDE, DORIS AND ARTHUR AND TOM WENT TO SCHOOL. MONTY WENT BACK TO SLEEP.

EVERY AFTERNOON, HE GAVE THEM A RIDE BACK.

...BUT MONTY
DID NOT COME.

THEN MONTY FLOATED BY.
MONTY! WHERE HAVE YOU BEEN?
I AM ON VACATION.
THIS IS NOT VACATION TIME!
IT IS FOR ME. THIS IS ALLIGATOR VACATION.

PARDON US FOR LIVING...

WHO WANTS TO WATCH A DUCK THINK, ANYWAY?

THAT'S ALL I NEED -- FOUR TURTLES...

...ALL I NEED?

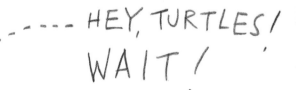

HEY, TURTLES! WAIT!

TURTLE NUMBER FOUR --- WHERE ARE YOU?

THEY WENT BACK TO SHORE, AND
PUT THEIR BOOKS IN THE SUN TO DRY.
TOM AND DORIS SAT DOWN.

HERE'S MY PLAN: YOU SIT ON THE BOARD, TOM.. AND I'LL JUMP OUT OF THE TREE ONTO THE OTHER END OF THE BOARD, AND YOU'LL GO FLYING RIGHT ACROSS THE RIVER!

THEY DECIDED TO TRY IT WITH DORIS BECAUSE SHE WAS THE LIGHTEST. DORIS STOOD ON THE BOARD.

BETTER,
BUT NOT PERFECT.

SPLASH

IT WAS CLEAR THAT THEY WOULD HAVE TO SWIM ACROSS.

WE THOUGHT YOU WERE ON VACATION...
I AM, BUT SOMETIMES WHEN I AM ON VACATION I TAKE A DAY OFF

THANKS FOR THE RIDE, MONTY!
IS THERE ANY CHANCE YOU'LL BE HERE THIS AFTERNOON, MONTY?
MONTY?
GUG... GUGGLE..
BUT MONTY HAD ALREADY STARTED TO SNORE.